Where would Father Christmas put the Christmas presents?

Normally Mr Happy helps Mr Forgetful to buy his tree, but this year Mr Happy had gone away for Christmas.

And now it was too late.

All the Christmas trees had been sold.

Everyone else had a tree.

Mr Greedy had bought his tree.

Mr Skinny had bought his tree.

Mr Mean had bought his tree.

And Mr Nonsense had bought six, just in case he ran out.

What nonsense!

Even Little Miss Late had a tree, although she had only got the very last one left.

Mr Forgetful realised that he had no choice but to go into the forest and cut down his own tree.

So, he set off through the snow.

Mr Forgetful walked and walked.

And walked some more.

But he could not find the perfect tree he was looking for.

They were too twisted.

Or too spindly.

Or too big.

"That won't fit in my living room," muttered Mr Forgetful.

After much searching he finally found a tree that was just right.

And it was then he realised he had forgotten his saw.

"Bother!" he said to himself. "I'll have to go back for it."

And it was then he realised that he had forgotten the way home!

Poor Mr Forgetful.

As he wandered through the forest trying to find his way home, he came upon some footprints in the snow.

"These must be my footprints," he guessed. "And if I follow them they should lead me back home."

But being the forgetful fellow he is, he forgot to follow them backwards and followed them forwards.

Back to the Christmas tree he had found!

Mr Forgetful was now in a terrible muddle.

As I'm sure you are. I know I am.

And he was cold.

And it was getting dark.

So he climbed a tree to see if he could see his house, but all he could see were trees.

And more trees.

In desperation he cried for help. **"HELP!"**

And as luck would have it, help was at hand.

Help in the form of Father Christmas who was flying over the forest in his sleigh at that very moment.

"I was just on my way to deliver your present to your house," said Father Christmas. "Would you like a lift?"

"By the way," asked Father Christmas, once they had arrived, "what were you doing up a tree in the middle of a forest on Christmas Eve?"

"You know what?" said Mr Forgetful. "I can't remember!"

"Now, where shall I put this?" asked Father Christmas, pulling a parcel out of his sack. A Christmas tree shaped parcel.

"Well I never," said Mr. Forgetful, suddenly remembering. "You are a marvel!"

Which just goes to show that Father Christmas really does know what everyone wants for Christmas.

Even if they've forgotten it themselves!